Silverlake Fairy School
Ready to Fly

Silverlake Fairy School

A magical world
where fairy dreams come true

Silverlake Fairy School

Ready to Fly

Elizabeth Lindsay

Illustrated by Anna Currey

USBORNE

For Katie F., with love

First published in 2009 by Usborne Publishing Ltd., Usborne House,
83-85 Saffron Hill, London EC1N 8RT, England.
www.usborne.com

Text copyright © Elizabeth Lindsay, 2009

Illustration copyright © Usborne Publishing Ltd., 2009

A CIP catalogue record for this book is available from the British Library.

UK ISBN 9780746090947 First published in America in 2011 AE.
American ISBN 9780794530648   JFM MJJASOND/11 01561/1
Printed in Dongguan, Guangdong, China.

Contents

Chapter One

The School Game

Lila's toes dangled above a giant dewflower. Her hair and fingernails perfectly matched the bloom's deep purple petals, although she didn't notice. She was far too busy watching the Silverlake Fairy School game; a Bugs and Butterflies match. It was so exciting it was all Lila could do not to join in.

The competitors were showing the First Year fairies how the game was played, and it had drawn such a crowd that Lila thought the whole school

Ready to Fly

must be watching. All four clan teams were playing and, as each fairy in the school belonged either to the Star, Sun, Moon or Cloud Clan, there was fierce rivalry. Every fairy wanted her clan team to win.

"Lila, look!"

Meggie, one of Lila's two best friends, pushed her yellow-ocher hair from her eyes and grasped Lila's arm. "Down there! It's a bug. It's so close. Can you see its poppy eyes? It's so hairy it's scary. The butterflies are so much nicer."

Lila, Meggie and the rest of the First Year class, Charm One, were seated on a viewing branch in one of the huge oak trees that surrounded the Bugs and Butterflies ring. Below them, in the ring, was a maze of giant flowers and shrubs that came from the seeds of a special silver sunflower that Mistress Pipit, the Charm One teacher, had planted in the center of the circle. With a wave of her wand, Mistress Pipit had scattered the magical

The School Game

seeds and they had transformed themselves into the lofty forest of plants and the special creatures, the bugs and the butterflies, that were required for the game.

The rules were easy to follow. Each player used her wand to tap the tails of as many bugs and butterflies as possible. The more bugs and butterflies caught, the higher the score. Each successful tap scored one team point. Fairies on opposing teams tried to catch each other too: a wand tap on the shoulder from a rival team member put a player out for the rest of the game. Naturally, as members of the Star Clan, Lila and Meggie were cheering for the Stars to win, but the Sun, Cloud and Moon supporters were cheering equally loudly.

"Look, it's Bella," cried Lila as three fairies chased one another above the foliage. Harebell, a sky-blue fairy, dropped down near the dewflower. "And she's seen a bug."

Ready to Fly

Bella was Lila's other best friend and Lila was proud that Bella played for the Stars. They watched her hide behind a clump of grasses and wait. When the bug finally peeked out from its hiding place a loud scream ripped the air and the bug disappeared. Bella dived after it and Lila leaned forward to see who had cried out.

"It was a wellipede," Princess Bee Balm said, laughing with her friend Sea Holly, but at the same time red with embarrassment. She tossed her pink hair proudly as she always did when she had made a mistake. It was obvious the scream had come from her. "Did you see its little boots?" the Princess continued. "It must have had a hundred little feet." Lila was surprised that any fairy could be scared of the bugs. They were harmless, magical creatures, part of a game.

"What are you staring at, Lilac Blossom?" said Bee Balm, crossly turning away. "Come on! Sun Clan! Sun Clan! We'll be the champions." But Lila

The School Game

had seen the look on Bee Balm's face; the bug *had* frightened her.

The petals on the dewflower trembled, and Meggie squeezed Lila's arm even tighter. The wellipede made a sudden dash for freedom but Bella was ready for it and touched the bug's tail with the star on the tip of her wand. The wellipede grunted crossly and vanished in a puff of sky-blue stars.

"That's Bella's fourth bug," Lila said, above the cheering. "She's a really good player."

"Yes," cried Meggie. "But I don't like the way the bugs wiggle."

"They're more scared of you than you are of them," said Lila. "They don't want to get caught. That's the fun of the game." But Lila could tell her friend wasn't convinced. Meggie was scared of the bugs too.

Pleased with her success, Bella flew skyward just as a Sun Clan fairy dropped down behind her,

Ready to Fly

with her wand ready to tap Bella's shoulder. Lila tensed; then, quite unexpectedly, Bella folded her wings and looped underneath her opponent, popping up sharply to tap the Sun Clan fairy's shoulder. The Sun Clan fairy was out.

"Boo, hiss, boo! Foul play, Harebell," cried Princess Bee Balm. "Boo, hiss, boo!"

Several surprised fairies turned toward the Princess. Lila ignored her and cheered and clapped loudly.

Alas, a trill of silver bells signaled that time was up. In a trice, all that was left of the game was a toadstool circle marking out a grassy ring. The flowers, tall grasses and shrubs, and the remaining bugs and butterflies, had all turned into little silver seeds once more. They returned to the magical Bugs and Butterflies sunflower that now stood alone in the center of the ring. The players fluttered, exhausted, onto the grass. Lila applauded loudly along with everyone else; she couldn't wait

to play her own game of Bugs and Butterflies and hoped it would be soon.

As Mistress Pipit collected the silver sunflower to take back into school, the players started chanting, "Pip-it, Pip-it, Pipity-Pip!" They wanted the result of the match. With a brief smile, the teacher called everyone onto the grass. All the fairies fluttered down eagerly to hear the score.

"That was a close-run game," said Mistress Pipit, folding her sparkling orange wings neatly. "The Moon Clan won with twenty-six points. Well done, Moons. Followed by the Sun Clan team with twenty-three points; the Star Clan came next with twenty-two and the Cloud Clan came fourth with twenty points."

There were cheers and claps for the winners but, underneath the applause, several distinct boos. Mistress Pipit held up her wand and every fairy fell silent.

"At Silverlake Fairy School we expect our pupils

to be good sports. I do not expect to hear any booing. We congratulate the winning team."

Princess Bee Balm pretended the boos hadn't come from her, and looked Mistress Pipit in the eye, but Sea Holly blushed, giving them both away. Mistress Pipit gave both fairies a sharp look before going over to speak to the winners.

Musk Mallow, a beautiful midnight-blue fairy, and the Star Clan's team captain, put her arm around Bella's shoulders, "Well done, Harebell," she said. "Shame we didn't win but it wasn't for want of trying. See you at the next practice, hey?" Then she fluttered off to talk to the older members of the team. Musk Mallow was also Deputy Head of the school *and* Head of the Star Clan. She was thought to be the best Bugs and Butterflies player in the whole school and, after watching her play, Lila could see why.

Bella stretched her wings and glowed with pleasure. She was the only player from Charm

Ready to Fly

One allowed to take part in the school game at present; the rest of the class had to pass the school's Flying Proficiency Test first. Bugs and Butterflies was Bella's one passion and playing for the Star Clan was all she cared about. As a result, her schoolwork had suffered and she had failed all her charm exams the previous year. Now she was having to do her entire first year all over again.

"The Suns beat the Stars, the Suns beat the Stars," chanted Princess Bee Balm behind her hand so no one but Lila, Bella and Meggie could hear.

"Take no notice, Bella," said Lila. "You played fantastically well."

But the Princess was quickly silenced by the return of Mistress Pipit.

"Check the seeds for me will you, Harebell?" she said, handing her the sunflower. "I think there's one missing."

The School Game

"Isn't it the best game ever?" Lila said to Meggie. "I can't wait for us to pass the flying test."

"I love the butterflies," Meggie replied. "They're beautiful and have such lovely colors. But the bugs…I know you keep telling me they're harmless. But look how high the podbugs can jump, and it's creepy how fast the wellipedes can run. I just don't like them."

"Scared of the bugs are we, Nutmeg?" said Bee Balm. "You would be."

"And what about you?" said Lila, sticking up for her friend. "You screamed when you saw the wellipede."

"I did not. I'd just broken a fingernail," said Bee Balm, hiding her hands behind her back. Lila knew she was lying. All the Princess's fingernails were immaculate.

Mistress Pipit waved her wand. "Line up, Charm One, we're returning to school for break.

Ready to Fly

When the bells ring for lessons, I want you to assemble by the Bewitching Pool."

Bella put up her hand. "Mistress Pipit, there *is* a seed missing."

"Ah, I thought so," said the teacher. "Let me have a look. Yes, it's a wellipede seed."

"Does that mean there's a wellipede missing?" Lila asked.

"I'm afraid it does, Lilac Blossom," Mistress Pipit replied. "It must have escaped before the game ended. But it'll turn up. If anyone sees it, touch its tail with your wand. It'll turn back into the missing seed and return to the sunflower."

"Watch out, Nutmeg, it's behind you," said Bee Balm, under her breath to Meggie.

Meggie spun around with a gasp. Bee Balm and Sea Holly giggled.

"Take no notice," said Bella. "The wellipede won't come anywhere near us. It knows we'll catch it if it does."

The School Game

"Miss 'Know-It-All' Harebell," hissed Bee Balm. "The fairy who failed all last year's charm exams. You and the yellow wimp fairy are perfect for Miss 'Pots-and-Pans' Lilac Blossom. Losers, all three of you!"

Bee Balm tossed her pink hair and, pulling Sea Holly with her, joined the line that gathered behind Mistress Pipit. Lila sighed. *The Princess may not like me but why does she have to be so horrible to my friends?*

Bee Balm hadn't wanted Lila to come to Silverlake Fairy School and had tried her best to make Lila fail the school entrance test. Lila had been a kitchen fairy at the Fairy Palace, and Bee Balm hated the idea of such a lowly fairy going to the same school as her own royal self. Fortunately, nobody else seemed to think the same way as Bee Balm and even the Fairy King and Queen had been thrilled when the school had accepted Lila. Thinking of home reminded Lila that she had left her letter to Cook and her best friend, Mip, in the Star Clan turret. "I'll mail it at lunchtime," she told herself.

As the line of fairies walked through the Wishing Wood to the garden, Lila let her mind race ahead to the next week, when the Charm One fairies were due to take their Flying Proficiency Test. After watching today's game, Lila was even more determined that both she and Meggie would pass first time. If they did, they would be free to fly alone and unsupervised, play Bugs and Butterflies whenever they had the opportunity and could even try for the Star Clan team.

Chapter Two

The Wishing Wood

When the bells finally trilled for the end of break Lila, Meggie and Bella gathered with the rest of Charm One beside the Bewitching Pool. Mistress Pipit arrived and held up her wand for silence.

"Now I hope you're feeling inspired after having seen your first Bugs and Butterflies game because it's time for us, as a class, to get down to some serious work." She paused and smiled. "You've done very well in our fairy gym lessons in

Ready to Fly

the garden. I think you're ready for the next step. Today, you're going to have your first flying lesson in the Flutter Tower."

"We're going to fly," cried Lila, jumping up and down. "At last, at last, at last!" Mistress Pipit gave Lila one of her quelling looks and Princess Bee Balm gave a haughty sniff in her direction, but Lila was too excited to care. From her bedroom window in the Star Clan turret, she had often looked at the Flutter Tower, standing higher than the tallest trees in the Wishing Wood and she longed to go inside it.

"Follow me," said Mistress Pipit, and set off with a line of eager fairies scurrying behind her. Lila couldn't have been happier and, chattering gaily, the three friends followed the other fairies through the trees of the Wishing Wood. Above them, the ancient oaks spread their mighty branches, shading out the sun, while long, sinewy roots anchored the great trunks to the earth.

The Wishing Wood

"Keep to the path," Mistress Pipit called back.

"It's rather gloomy, isn't it?" Meggie said. "It feels as though that escaped wellipede might drop from one of the branches at any minute."

"It won't," said Bella. "Wellipedes are no good at climbing. It's podbugs that leap into things."

"Pipity isn't going to make us fly to the very top of the Flutter Tower, is she?" Meggie asked. "Heights make me dizzy. Even looking out of our bedroom window makes me freeze. There, I've said it."

"Dizzy!" said Bella as if she couldn't believe her ears. "But fairies have to fly high, that's what we do. In Year Five we'll be learning to collect stardust."

"I know," Meggie said, miserably. "But maybe by then I won't be so frightened. I just don't want to have to go too high in the Flying Test. That's all."

Ahead of them, Princess Bee Balm whispered something in Sea Holly's ear. Both fairies glanced back and giggled.

Ready to Fly

"Butterburs and bodkins!" Lila grimaced. "Bee Balm's eavesdropping again!"

Waiting until the Princess and Sea Holly were out of hearing, Bella continued: "Meggie, how can you possibly be scared of heights? Flying high and free is fantastic fun."

"Bella!" scolded Lila. "Just because you're the sporty type and not scared of anything! Meggie may not like heights but she's good at lots of other things."

The sky-blue fairy looked sheepish.

"You mustn't worry about the test, Meggie," Lila said. "We'll do lots and lots of practice."

Ahead, Mistress Pipit stopped and turned to the fairies following her. "I'd like you all to listen carefully," she said. "The Wishing Wood is full of pathways and until you've learned them you must keep together. We're on one of the main routes, but here, at this oak tree, the path forks. The left path eventually takes you back to the Bugs and

The Wishing Wood

Butterflies ring, where we were earlier. Don't use this path if you're in a hurry."

"That's for sure," whispered Bella, who knew the pathways like the back of her hand.

"The right fork leads to the Flutter Tower. Now, keep together. Bella and Lila, please can you stay at the back and make sure nobody goes the wrong way."

"Hey, Meggie, stay with us," Bella said.

"I can't think why you'd want her to," said Bee Balm. "A fairy who doesn't like heights isn't much of a fairy, is she?"

"A princess should be above making unpleasant remarks," said Lila, jumping in. "Don't you want your subjects to be loyal to you if you become queen?"

"It's not *if* I become queen but *when*, Lilac Blossom," said Bee Balm, ignoring the important part of what Lila had said. "Now tootle to the back of the line you three, where you belong."

Ready to Fly

"She is such a snob," said Bella, making a face behind the Princess's back.

The path ahead twisted and turned and sunlight dappled their way. Birds sang merrily in the trees, red squirrels jumped from branch to branch, and nobody got left behind. At last, Charm One arrived at the base of a glittering silver tower. It was higher than the trees and, from where they were standing, it was impossible to see the top.

"How do we get in?" Lila asked. "There's no door."

"Wait and see," said Bella.

Mistress Pipit ran her eye over the class to check that everyone was there.

"This is the Flutter Tower," she announced. "It must only be used with Day Lily, our dear Head Fairy, any of the four Head of Clan fairies, or with a teacher in attendance. You must not come in here by yourselves. Is that understood?"

Ready to Fly

"Yes, Mistress Pipit," murmured the class. Everyone in Charm One looked up to Day Lily. She was a beautiful, vibrant yellow fairy and almost as grown up as the teachers. She and Musk Mallow were best friends and Lila thought they were both wonderful.

"Once inside I want you all to wait quietly and keep both feet on the ground," Mistress Pipit continued. "When you've all passed the Flying Proficiency Test we will fly in at the top of the tower. But today we'll go in this way."

Mistress Pipit raised her orange wand and a dazzling spark shot from the sun at its tip and hit the silver wall. A door appeared and opened invitingly. Full of curiosity, the class followed Mistress Pipit inside. The door closed behind them and vanished.

The Flutter Tower, Lila quickly realized, was a special kind of gymnasium, with trapeze bars and walkways, ladders and ropes crisscrossing into the air. There were galleries, ledges and balconies around the walls and the roof was made of silver branches woven into a canopy, as though they were trees in the Wishing Wood. At the center of the canopy was a hole where sunlight poured through, lighting up the inside of the tower.

"Divide into Clans, please," said Mistress Pipit. "Stars, Moons, Suns and Clouds find each other quickly."

Lila, Meggie and Bella would be together, with the three other Star Clan members in the class, Cowslip, Periwinkle and Primrose. Mistress Pipit clapped her hands and, from between the silver branches above, four fairies came fluttering down to join them.

"As it's our first lesson in the Flutter Tower, Musk Mallow, Marigold, Angelica and Campion are going to be your team leaders," said Mistress Pipit. There were delighted smiles from the class who applauded their Head of Clan fairies with enthusiasm.

Ready to Fly

Bee Balm carefully arranged her pink gossamer frock and smiled sweetly at Marigold, head of the Sun Clan. But Marigold was too busy counting her team and lining them up to notice. In a huff, Bee Balm pushed in next to Sea Holly and the others gave way as usual.

"Honestly, did you see that?" whispered Lila. "Bee Balm thinks she rules the whole class."

"She *thinks* she does, but she doesn't," Bella whispered back.

"Quite," said Meggie. "She doesn't *rule* us."

"Stop talking you three and line up," said Musk Mallow, ushering the Star fairies into place. "Now, pay attention to Mistress Pipit."

"I want you to listen carefully, Charm One," their teacher told them. "Because I have several important things to tell you before we begin."

Lila was all ears. She was desperate to get flying and the Flutter Tower looked like the most wonderful fun. The sooner they started the better.

Chapter Three

The Flutter Tower

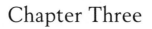

Mistress Pipit gave Charm One a list of rules that, to Lila's ears, seemed to go on forever. They were not to race, not to push or chase and had to take turns doing everything. They were to look out for one another and to encourage each other. Anyone who fell, she explained, would be caught by the safety nets. That intrigued Lila, as she couldn't see any nets and guessed they were part of the Flutter Tower's magic. Wands were to be left by the wall so they didn't get broken.

Ready to Fly

Finally, Mistress Pipit asked Musk Mallow to step forward.

"Right, everyone," Musk Mallow said. "Before we begin, Harebell is going to give us a demonstration of what each fairy must do to pass the Flying Proficiency Test."

"Easy peasy." Bella grinned, surprised but pleased to have been chosen.

"Afterward, we'll practice in our clan groups. There are six different parts, or maneuvers, as we call them, to the test. But, that's all right, you'll have plenty of time to learn them. We Head of Clan fairies will bring you into the Flutter Tower to make sure you get plenty of practice and so will Day Lily, if she has time. Okay, Bella. Maneuver one, please."

Bella flew vertically into the air, rising straight up, until she reached the silver branches where she chose a resting place and sat down.

"You have to stay on a branch for a count of

three," said Musk Mallow, signaling with her wand for Bella to fly down again.

"That looks easy enough," Lila whispered to Meggie.

"It's very high up," came the nervous reply.

"Second maneuver, please, Bella," said Musk Mallow.

Once again, Bella shot skyward and flew to some handholds near the top of the wall, held on and stayed absolutely still.

"Once you let go, you have to free fall to a count of three," continued Musk Mallow, signaling. Bella dived head first, counted, "One, two, three," then opened her wings and flew. Lila thought that looked scary and difficult.

The third maneuver was to fly to a trapeze bar, swing and jump, hover and drop. For the fourth maneuver Bella stood on a ladder, caught a ball and threw it up in the air again and for the fifth, she hovered, knotting a rope to the ladder, without letting her feet touch the rungs once. There was a lot to remember and Bella was so graceful she made each task appear much simpler than it really was.

The sixth and final maneuver had to be done with a partner. Musk Mallow took Bella's hand and the two fairies flew into the air together, separating to sit on opposite trapeze bars, facing each other. They swung backward and forward until their toes touched. With the next swing, both fairies pushed off from their bars, and with a flying twist, landed on the bar their partner had just left.

"They've changed places," gasped Lila. "And made it look easy."

"We'll never be able to do that," said Meggie. "Will we?"

As the bars swung together Bella and Musk Mallow slipped from their seats, took hands, and together fluttered earthward turning two perfect somersaults before landing on their toes, still hand in hand. They were greeted with an enthusiastic round of applause.

Meggie shook her head. "No, we'll never be able to do that!"

"We will," said Lila. "We certainly will."

Princess Bee Balm was frowning, that is, until her glance met Lila's, when she composed herself. *Well*, Lila thought. Bee Balm's always making fun of Bella for failing her charm exams but she'll never fly as well as that and I think she knows it.

Musk Mallow smiled encouragingly at her group of fairies. "There's lots to learn," she said. "But don't be discouraged. Let's get practicing. Who thinks they can fly as high as the silver branches?" Everyone put up a hand, even Meggie. "And who wants to go first?" All the hands went down except Lila's. "Okay, Lilac Blossom. First maneuver. Can you remember it?"

Lila nodded.

"Off you go then and do your best."

Ready to Fly

Lila stretched out her wings and took off. Fairies from the other clans were already in the air above her. One of them was Bee Balm. Lila spiraled round and round getting higher and higher as she flew. The maneuver was much harder than it looked. She wasn't sure how Bella had managed to go up in a straight line, but at least she was getting there. Bee Balm, red with exertion, was taking a rest on a trapeze bar.

"Keep going up, Bee Balm," shouted Marigold. "Don't stop!"

"I'll stop if I want to," muttered the Princess. "Show off!" she sneered as Lila flew past.

Puffed but nearly there, Lila fluttered onto a silver branch and looked down. For a moment she felt giddy. Everyone below appeared very small. It made her realize how tall the Flutter Tower really was. Musk Mallow gave her the signal and she plunged down. She took care not to descend too fast and landed safely on her toes.

Ready to Fly

"Well done," said Musk Mallow. "Who's next?" The others still hung back.

"I'll go," said Meggie, her face pale.

"You can do it," whispered Lila. "I know you can."

"I must try before I lose my nerve." Meggie flew up slowly and steadily and kept her eyes on her destination. Bee Balm, seeing Meggie approach, slid off the trapeze and flew ahead to claim the lowest of the silver branches. Meggie found a perch higher up, but the moment she looked down she froze. Bee Balm fluttered to the ground with a superior smile.

"Nutmeg's gone as rigid as a stick," she said. "How she ever thinks she'll pass the test, I don't know. A fairy scared of heights. Ridiculous!"

"We must help her," said Lila, shooting into the air. "Come on, Bella."

Lila and Bella flew up as fast as they could, but Musk Mallow quickly overtook them and reached the silver branch first. Meggie's eyes were glassy with fear.

"I can't move," she rasped.

"Listen," said Musk Mallow, putting a comforting arm around her, "no harm can come to you in here even if you do fall. A net will always catch you. Show her, Bella."

"It's terrific fun, too," said Bella, folding her wings and falling. She had gone hardly any distance when a net appeared under her and she bounced into it. She fluttered back up and the net disappeared. "See, the charms make it perfectly safe to fall. You can't hurt yourself."

"Take my hand, Meggie," said Musk Mallow. "We'll go down together."

"Yes," Meggie gulped. "I must be brave."

Musk Mallow's calm presence gave Meggie the confidence to slip from the branch and, by the time she was halfway to the floor, she let go of her clan leader's hand and fluttered the rest of the way by herself.

"Well done, Nutmeg!" said Musk Mallow. Bee Balm looked scornful. She didn't think Meggie had done well at all.

"In the end, it was much easier than I imagined," Meggie whispered to Lila. "Once I got over the shock of how far down the ground was."

After that, Meggie became more relaxed and enjoyed the challenge of the other exercises. Yet try as they might, neither Lila, nor Meggie could hover and tie the rope, or turn somersaults holding hands, but Bella gave them a pleased wink when the practice was over and Musk Mallow called them all to the ground.

"Well done, Stars. I'm proud of you. I know some of you found it difficult today, but practice hard and you should all pass the test."

On hearing Musk Mallow's praise Lila's confidence grew and so did Meggie's.

"I didn't think I'd be able to do *any* of it," said

The Flutter Tower

Meggie. "But I can. Knowing there are nets to catch me if I slip or fall really helps."

"Nets," scoffed Bee Balm, eavesdropping again. "You won't always have nets to catch you."

"Meggie knows that," said Lila. "Give her a chance."

"You can stick up for your little friend all you like," grimaced Bee Balm. "But if she can't fly properly she shouldn't be at Silverlake Fairy School."

"Meggie does fly properly," said Lila. "And she'll pass the test, you wait and see."

"I doubt it!" scoffed the Princess. "But we'll soon find out."

When the Princess was out of earshot Bella said, "It's strange that Bee Balm thinks she's more skillful than everyone else. You and Meggie can fly so much better than she can."

"Me better than Bee Balm?" said Meggie, surprised.

Ready to Fly

"You fly very well when you're not scared," said Bella.

"See, Meggie," said Lila. "That's real praise coming from Bella."

On the walk back through the Wishing Wood to the garden, Lila's thoughts drifted to wondering whether she'd ever be good enough to get into the Star Clan's Bugs and Butterflies team. Bella was the only First Year player. The rest of the team was made up with Fourth and Fifth Year fairies. Lila decided she would work hard at her flying every day and help Meggie to do the same. She was hopeful that with lots of practice, they would both pass the Flying Test. Afterward, with luck, and a lot of hard work, she might even make it into the Bugs and Butterflies team. It would be a real challenge.

Chapter Four

Trouble

"It's just as well it's nearly lunchtime," said Bella, as they reached the garden. "I'm starving."

Meggie flopped onto the grass, tired after all the flying, and closed her eyes. "What bliss! I won't move until the lunch bells ring," she said.

"I'm going to the refectory to get in line," said Bella. "I'll save you fairies a place."

"Thanks, Bella," said Meggie dreamily, as Bella fluttered off.

Ready to Fly

"I think I'll mail my letter now," said Lila.

"I'll wait here for you then," Meggie said, hardly stirring.

Bee Balm and Sea Holly were sitting further off, with their heads together and their eyes on Lila.

"Okay," said Lila and, keeping her feet firmly on the ground and her wings neatly folded, she walked briskly toward the Hall of Rainbows. The school rules said "No Flying" until you passed the Flying Proficiency Test and Lila was not going to risk getting into trouble now, especially when Bee Balm and Sea Holly were eager for her to make a mistake.

Lila was in the Star Clan turret, adding a P.S. to her letter, all about the Bugs and Butterflies game and the Flutter Tower, when the lunch bells rang.

"Butterburs and bodkins," she said, dotting kisses everywhere, and rolling up the letter-scroll.

Trouble

"Now I'll have to run."

She whizzed down the Owl staircase, dodged fairies in the Hall of Rainbows, and burst into the sunshine. Meggie was dozing on the grass. Lila didn't disturb her and ran toward the gatehouse. *I'll wake her up on the way back*, Lila thought.

Captain Klop was the gruff dragon in charge of the mail. All letters were to be taken to him. He was also the Silverlake Fairy School gatekeeper. Lila, along with all the other First Year fairies, was a little scared of him.

She crossed the silver cobbles to Captain Klop's door but couldn't see anywhere to put her letter, so she knocked and waited. And waited. Nothing happened. Lila was torn; should she go or should she stay? At this rate she and Meggie wouldn't get any lunch. But at last, the latch clicked, and the door opened.

Captain Klop had the battered look of a dragon who had been in many a fight. His right ear was torn and a front tooth broken. His drooping lip curled into a snarl.

"Yes, what do you want?"

"Excuse me, Captain Klop," said Lila, curtsying politely. "Please may I mail this letter to the Fairy Palace kitchen?"

The dragon peered down his nose and narrowed his eyes.

"Put any letters in the basket over there. The doves take the mail at four sharp every day, weather permitting."

Lila followed the direction of the dragon's claw and saw that he was pointing to a basket that hung underneath a hovering blue and white balloon. Above the balloon, six white doves dozed along a rafter. But now, one by one, they opened their eyes and cooed for some birdseed.

"Greedy birds," said the dragon, turning to go back in. "You'll have food when you come home again tomorrow."

Trouble

"Excuse me, please," said Lila again.

"Now what?" asked the dragon.

"It's just that I haven't yet passed the Flying Proficiency Test and I can't reach the basket from the ground. Please, will you put my letter in for me?"

The dragon gave Lila a more interested look.

"You're Cook's little fairy, aren't you? Should have thought, you being purple an' all. Not many fairies your color about." He leaned down and took the scroll from Lila. "How are things going, Lilac Blossom?"

"Very well, thank you," said Lila, delighted that he remembered her name.

"And what's it like being in the same class as Princess Bee Balm? I imagine she can be a handful. Treating you well, I hope?"

"Oh, yes," said Lila, not knowing what else to say. She couldn't possibly tell him that the Princess was the meanest person she had ever met.

Ready to Fly

The old dragon limped over to the balloon and dropped Lila's letter into the basket.

"It'll be delivered tonight," said Captain Klop, "unless it's raining. We can't be doing with soggy letters, now, can we? Off you go then. The bells have gone for lunch."

"Thank you very much," said Lila, curtsying again before hurrying away. Captain Klop watched her go with interest.

Lila ran toward the Bewitching Pool to discover that the garden was deserted. Meggie must have gone in to lunch without her. She was halfway toward the Hall of Rainbows when someone called out her name. It was Sea Holly running toward her from the Wishing Wood.

"Your friend Nutmeg's stuck up a tree," Sea Holly told her.

"She can't be," said Lila. "I left her dozing by the Bewitching Pool. She's gone in to lunch."

"Well, someone's up there sobbing their heart

Trouble

out. It sounds like Nutmeg to me," said Sea Holly. "I'm going to get help." Sea Holly hurried on into school as if she was on the most important mission of her life.

*Why in the name of stars and moons would Meggie have climbed into a tree? Unless...*and Lila gasped at the possibility. "Unless, she's been frightened by the missing wellipede!"

Lila wasted no more time and hurried into the Wishing Wood to find her. Sobs were coming from somewhere high up in a nearby oak. She ran to the foot of the tree and peered between the branches. A tingle on her wrist made her take hold of the little silver unicorn – her first day charm – on her school bracelet. She wasn't sure what to do. She wanted to get into the tree but the no-flying rule prevented her. She wished the silver unicorn would come to life and tell her what to do.

"Meggie," she called up. "Is that you? Are you stuck? Meggie, it's me, Lila."

Trouble

The sobbing became louder and more distressed. The little unicorn tingled again. What was it trying to tell her?

"Listen, Meggie, stop crying. Sea Holly's gone for help. I'll go and hurry everyone up."

"Don't l-l-leave me. Please, don't go. I'm going to f-f-fall," choked the sobbing voice.

The unicorn tingled again, more urgently. *It must want me to help!* thought Lila. "Don't move," she called. "I'm coming. Stay exactly where you are."

Lila tried to climb the tree but none of the branches was low enough even if she jumped her highest. There was nothing left to do. She spread her wings and flew to the first large bough. Then, half climbing, half fluttering, she went on up. "I'm coming. Just hold on," she cried. Silence. Not a leaf fluttered or a branch swayed. "Meggie? Meggie, where are you?"

There was no one at the top of the tree. But how could that be? She'd heard the sobbing.

Ready to Fly

Sea Holly had heard it too. *Oh no! Oh, no, no, no, no no!* Lila had the most dreadful thought and another urgent tingle on her wrist sent her flying down between the branches like a whirlwind. She dived from the bottom bough, landing on the ground in a breathless, crumpled heap.

She wasn't alone. Mistress Pipit was staring down at her with astonishment. Behind the teacher were Meggie, Bella and Musk Mallow, each looking equally surprised. Behind them stood Bee Balm and Sea Holly, barely attempting to hide their gleeful smirks.

"I thought Meggie was stuck in the tree." Lila could hardly get the words out. "At least, that's what Sea Holly told me."

"I did not," said Sea Holly, pretending surprise. "I saw you in the tree and went to get help." With that lie, Lila knew she was done for.

"That's enough," said Mistress Pipit, holding up her orange wand and looking from one to the

Trouble

other. "Lilac Blossom, I'm very disappointed in you. I do not take rule-breaking lightly."

"I'm sorry, Mistress Pipit," said Lila, her voice a whisper, as she took hold of the little unicorn. It had been trying to warn her not to fly. If only she had understood it.

"Of course," continued Mistress Pipit, "if a fairy had been stuck in the tree I could have been lenient, but Nutmeg was in the refectory along with the rest of Charm One. I'm afraid there's nothing to be done. Lose six clan points and you'll wait an extra two weeks to take the Flying Proficiency Test. If you break the no-flying rule one more time, you won't take the test until next term. Is that understood?"

"Yes, Mistress Pipit." Lila knew it was useless to argue. Instead she blushed a deep purple at the shame and injustice of it all.

"Now come along to the refectory at once and have your lunch, which is what you should have been doing in the first place."

Lila trailed miserably after her teacher. She didn't feel at all like eating. She had let the Star Clan down by losing six clan points. Six! Bee Balm and Sea Holly were practically dancing back to the refectory. They had carried out the perfect trick. And, because of them, Lila couldn't take the Flying Test. Worse still, Mistress Pipit thought that she had told a lie, and that Sea Holly's made-up story was true. It was so unfair.

Chapter Five

Trick

At last, Lila was able to get away from the refectory and return to the garden. Meggie and Bella pounced on her the moment she appeared.

"Lila, what happened?" they wanted to know.

"I was so stupid," Lila cried, shaking her head. "Everything I told Pipity was true. I'd given my letter to Captain Klop and was going back into school when Sea Holly ran from the Wishing Wood saying Meggie was stuck in a tree.

And there was somebody up there. I heard them sobbing."

"Oh, Lila," said Meggie. "If only I hadn't listened to Bee Balm. She woke me up and told me everyone had gone in to lunch, including you. I thought maybe you hadn't heard me say I'd wait for you."

"A neat little trick," said Bella. "Bee Balm and Sea Holly must be laughing themselves silly."

"But what I don't understand is the sobbing," said Lila. "And the voice crying, 'Don't leave me. Please, don't go. I'm going to fall.' It sounded just like you, Meggie, and it came from the top of the tree." Lila sighed with exasperation. "I'd never have flown up there unless it was really important. But the stupidest thing of all was that my silver unicorn tried to warn me. It tingled three times. I wish I'd understood why."

"Well it's easy to know the answer after something's happened," said Bella. "Next time it tingles you'll know it means 'watch out'."

Trick

"That's for sure," said Lila, slumping to the ground, "but what am I going to do now?"

"Don't let them get away with it," said Bella. "We've got to work this out step by step."

Lila sat up again. "Yes, we must." She was thinking hard. "Was Bee Balm in the refectory when Sea Holly told everyone I was in the tree?"

"No, no she wasn't," said Meggie, remembering. "Bee Balm told me the bells had rung but didn't come in to lunch herself."

"Well, well," said Bella. "The plot thickens."

"But she was there when we found you at the oak tree," Meggie added. "That's when I next remember seeing her."

"Which means," said Bella. "She could have been up the tree pretending to be you, Meggie."

"No, that doesn't explain it. How come I got so close I could have touched the person sobbing, but there was nobody there?" asked Lila.

"Sounds like some sort of magic," said Bella.

Ready to Fly

"That's it!" said Lila. "That's the answer."

"What? What did I say?"

"I think Bee Balm's learned a special charm," said Lila.

"An invisibility charm?" suggested Meggie.

"No, no, I don't think it was an invisibility charm. Nothing moved, not a branch, not a leaf, nothing. And I didn't hear a single rustle. It's something else."

"A crying charm?" Meggie asked.

"But there were words as well," Lila said. "Is there such a thing as a charm where you can speak in one place and your voice is heard in another? If there is, Bee Balm wouldn't have had to be at the top of the tree to trick me."

"Wait," said Bella. "It's coming back to me. I'm sure we did this last year. It's got a special name."

"A voice-sending charm?" suggested Lila.

"Oh, bats' umbrellas...I can't remember," said Bella. "I'm sorry. But I do remember Bee Balm boasting the other day that since she got a place at Silverlake the Lord Chamberlain had let her make charms with his wand. I bet she knows a few things we don't."

"The Lord Chamberlain's really clever," said Meggie. "He's probably taught Bee Balm some advanced charms."

"Please, try and remember the name of this voice charm, Bella," said Lila, trying not to get distracted. "Then we can look it up and find out if it is what Bee Balm used."

"I just can't remember," said Bella. "But it might be in *Charms for Beginners*. You know, that whopping book in the library, with everything in it you're supposed to know by the end of the First Year."

"What are we waiting for?" said Lila, jumping up. "If a charm like that exists it could prove my story was true."

She raced across the grass into the Hall of

Ready to Fly

Rainbows, where her speed took her slithering to the library door. Meggie and Bella caught up to Lila beside a sign that read "Silence" in large imposing letters.

"Be careful," said Bella. "If old Thorny's in there, she's a stickler for no talking, and takes away clan points like anything."

"You mean the librarian, Mistress Hawthorn?" said Meggie. "Yes, I thought she looked scary."

"Bella, you'd better get *Charms for Beginners*," said Lila. "You know where to find it."

"Me? I don't have a clue where it is," said Bella.

"But didn't you use it last year?" asked Meggie.

Bella blushed a glowing sky-blue and looked at her toes. "I've seen other fairies use it."

"Oh Bella!" said Meggie. "No wonder you failed all your charm exams."

"Well, that's about to change," said Lila, giving the vaulted door a determined push. She was met with a musty smell of dust and leather polish. She remembered it from the library at the Fairy Palace. The room was grand and gloomy. Dark wooden steps and little balconies wound around and around the book-lined walls leading up and up to a high, painted ceiling. Lila looked about her in awe. There were thousands of volumes, with many different-colored spines covered in gold and silver writing. Library elves were busy polishing some of the covers. How would they ever find *Charms for Beginners* from among so many books?

Lila lowered her eyes from the ceiling and met the alarming gaze of Mistress Hawthorn, a leaf-green fairy with white wing tips. The librarian peered at Lila over round spectacles that perched on the end of her nose. Lila tiptoed to the desk where Mistress Hawthorn, surrounded by several large leather bound volumes, raised her eyebrows questioningly and waited.

Trick

"Please, Mistress Hawthorn," whispered Lila. "May we borrow *Charms for Beginners*?"

"You may look at it here but you may not remove it from the library," Mistress Hawthorn said, giving Lila an appraising look. "It's a reference book. You'll find it over there on the bottom shelf. Good to see you making a voluntary visit to the library, Harebell," she added. "I hope we'll be seeing more of you this year."

Lila curtsied her thanks, Bella blushed again and the three friends hurried over to find the book. Lila ran her wand along the line of volumes: *Charms for Gardens and Woods*; *Charms and Fairy Gold*; *Charms and Dream Wishes* and, at last, *Charms for Beginners*. She shoved her wand in her waistband and pulled the book from the shelf.

The cover was made of purple leather with the title embossed in golden letters on the front and the spine.

Ready to Fly

"Wow," Lila whispered. "It's written by Fairy Godmother Whimbrel." The book now felt really special. "Do you think all the book covers are given the same fairy color as their authors?"

"Maybe," whispered Bella. "I've never noticed before."

"That's not surprising," said Lila, heaving the book onto the nearest table. "If you never come into the library."

"All right, all right," muttered Bella. "But I've always had other things to do."

Meggie gave Lila a dig. Mistress Hawthorn was giving them a beady stare, but right now Lila didn't care. She turned the pages excitedly. The charms were listed alphabetically. Lila turned to the letter V for voice. There were charms to lose voices, to bring back voices, to make voices louder or softer but there was absolutely nothing about a *voice-sending* charm.

"It's not here," she whispered.

Trick

"It must be," said Bella.

"It's not under voice," Lila said. "It must start with something else and we don't have time to go through the whole book. Think, Bella."

Bella closed her eyes, trying her hardest to recall something she had only the vaguest memory of. Lila tapped her fingers impatiently and Meggie slowly turned back the pages of the book.

"I'm sure it began with a V," Bella said. "V... vin...ven something."

"Ventriloquism?" whispered Meggie, pointing.

"That's it," said Bella.

Lila poured over the page.

"It says here, 'the ventriloquism charm is a wand spell for throwing the voice'. Sending the voice, throwing the voice, it's the same thing, isn't it? This charm might be it." She took her rainbow pencil and notes' scroll from her pocket, wrote down the page number so they could find it again if they needed to and started to copy out the charm. She had almost finished when the bells rang for afternoon classes.

"You two go," she said. "I'll come when I've finished."

"You'll get into more trouble if you're late," said Meggie. "Let me do it."

"No, it's nearly done and I'm learning it as I write."

"Come on," said Bella, taking Meggie by the hand. "There's no point in us all losing clan points. We won't have any left at this rate."

Lila hurried to finish. It took her another few minutes but it was worth it. She slammed the book shut, reminding Mistress Hawthorn that she was still in the library. A kindly elf took the book from her and put it back on the shelf.

"Lilac Blossom, go," said Mistress Hawthorn. "You're late for class!"

"Sorry," said Lila, scurrying to the door and pocketing the notes' scroll as she went. She raced

Trick

down the Hall of Rainbows and up the Swallow staircase and fairly whizzed along the orange corridor to her classroom. She flung herself through the door just as everyone else was sitting down. Ignoring Bee Balm's mocking smile she hurried to her mushroom desk where she sat down, panting. Right now nothing mattered more than proving her innocence. She was desperate to take the Flying Proficiency Test with the rest of the class. It was all that mattered.

Chapter Six

Ventriloquism

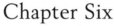

Later that evening, when the day was almost over, Lila, Bella and Meggie had a secret meeting in their bedroom in the Star Clan turret. Lila had her notes' scroll and her wand ready.

"I'm going to try out the ventriloquism charm," she announced. "It'll be useful to know how it works. Anyone else want to try it?"

"You bet," said Bella. "What about you, Meggie?"

"Okay, but we mustn't let Bee Balm and Sea Holly know we can do it," said Meggie.

Ventriloquism

"Absolutely not," Lila agreed, studying her notes to work out how to do the charm. "Now you've got to touch the lips of the speaker with the wand tip and flick the wrist. That sets the charm going. Then point the wand in the direction you want the voice to go. To keep the voice moving, flick the wand backward and forward. Sounds simple enough. Here goes."

Lila touched her lips and flicked her wrist.

"Buzz, buzz, buzz," she said, waving her wand. The first buzz came from her mouth as usual. The second two buzzes came from her right foot. Lila laughed and flicked her wand again and re-touched her lips. "Buzz, buzz buzz," she said again. Her voice was back to normal. "Well, it's easy to stop the charm but I don't understand why my voice came from my toes, when I wanted it to come from the window."

"It almost worked though," said Bella.

"I suppose so."

Ready to Fly

"Let me try," said Meggie.

Meggie went through the same process and her buzzes went nowhere at all. Neither did Bella's when she tried.

"It's really difficult," said Bella, dropping her wand on the table with a frown. But Lila wasn't going to give up.

"Close your eyes," she said. "When you hear a buzz, point to where you think it's coming from."

Lila touched her lips with the wand and flicked her wrist. Concentrating hard, she directed her voice.

"Buzz, buzz, buzz, you can't catch me."

Both Meggie and Bella pointed their wands to the ceiling. When they opened their eyes they were impressed to find Lila was sitting on her bed.

"Hey, I'm getting it. It's the flick of the wrist that does it," said Lila, forgetting to direct her

Ventriloquism

voice, so that it drifted across the room and came out of Bella's mouth. Bella got the giggles and so did Lila. They laughed even more when Lila's voice chuckled out from Meggie's knees.

"Get a grip, Lila," said Bella, when she could speak again.

Lila aimed her wand more accurately. "I'm flying near the ceiling! Round and around I go," she said, her mouth opening and closing silently, while the sound of her voice flew through the air above them.

"Can you hear me? I'm up here." Lila appeared to be talking from the top of the wardrobe. "No, I'm here." Then her voice came from the window, "No, down here!" and under the bed. Laughing, Lila undid the charm. "I'm going to practice this loads. It's great fun."

"I wish I could do it," Bella grinned.

"You can," said Lila. "Come on, you two, start practicing."

Ventriloquism

Soon all kinds of sounds could be heard. A piggy grunting noise came from near the top of the door. That was Bella. Meggie lay on top of her bed and made barking come from underneath it while Lila sent her voice bouncing all over the room. She even made it come from Meggie's wand, which had Bella doubled up with laughter.

The door opened and the practice came to an abrupt stop as Musk Mallow walked in.

"What's all the noise in here?" she demanded. "You three should be ready for bed, it's late." There was a scramble to get into nightdresses. When all three fairies were sitting ready on their beds, Musk Mallow said, "I've put up a notice about the next Bugs and Butterflies practice. It's the day after the Flying Test. I hope that the Stars who pass will try for the team. I saw some excellent flying this morning."

"Musk Mallow, I'm sorry but I can't be there," said Lila, hating to admit it.

Ready to Fly

"So I heard," said the Head of Clan fairy.

"And I've lost six Star Clan points." Lila looked down, ashamed. "I'll try and make them up again, really I will."

"I heard something about you flying up into a tree to rescue Meggie, but she wasn't there. It didn't seem to make sense."

"It was a trick," said Bella. "We know who did it. Lila really did think Meggie was stuck."

"A trick?" Musk Mallow said. "Who tricked you?"

Lila gave Bella a warning stare. She wasn't sure she wanted Musk Mallow to know how foolish she had been made to look.

"Bee Balm and Sea Holly," said Bella, ignoring Lila. "Bee Balm's constantly trying to get Lila into trouble and this time she's succeeded."

Musk Mallow nodded sympathetically, and Lila felt encouraged to explain what had happened.

"The thing is it's my word against Sea Holly's,"

Ventriloquism

she said. "And, because Meggie was in the refectory, everyone thinks I was lying."

"We know it was a deliberate trick because Bee Balm told me Lila had gone in to lunch when she hadn't," said Meggie. "And they both looked so pleased when Lila was caught flying."

"And Sea Holly told a lie too," said Bella. "But we're going to prove Lila's innocence."

"Please, don't get yourselves into more trouble over this," Musk Mallow said. "But if I can help at all, let me know. Okay?"

"Thanks, Musk Mallow," said Lila, gratefully.

"Oh, and before I forget, flying practices will be after lunch every day until the test and in the evenings as well. I want to see you at all of them. Is that understood, Stars?"

"Yes, Musk Mallow," they chanted.

"And I mean it, Lilac Blossom, if you need help with anything, just ask. Now, into bed."

When the light was turned out, Lila puzzled

Ready to Fly

over ways of making Bee Balm and Sea Holly confess to the trick they had pulled, but nothing came to her and she tossed and turned in frustration. Soon the whole school would know she was banned from taking the Flying Test. It was a humiliating thought.

The next morning Lila woke up miserable and despairing. Meggie gave her a big hug and Bella said, "Don't worry, Lila. The truth always comes out in the end. You wait and see." But waiting and seeing was difficult if you were the sort of fairy who wanted to take action. And how long would she have to wait? Lila wanted to solve the problem right away.

Chapter Seven

Practice Makes Perfect

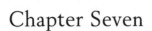

The following few days were busy for Lila and her friends. There were a lot of simple wand charms to learn and Mistress Pipit was eager for them to learn more. Lila's favorite charm was giving out the quills, which she could now do with a simple dip of her wand tip. It gave her great pleasure to watch the white feather pens flutter through the air and land, one on each desk. Then there was all the extra practicing for the Flying Proficiency Test. Musk Mallow's encouragement and patience made it easy for the Stars. She also offered Meggie extra help, first thing in the morning, to overcome her fear of heights.

"Isn't Musk Mallow kind?" Meggie said, after her first session. "She gave me the courage to fly over the garden and up to a branch in the Wishing Wood. I didn't get scared once with her flying by my side."

Bella helped Musk Mallow with the Star Clan sessions in the Flutter Tower, trying her hardest to get Lila and Meggie to turn accurate somersaults. There was much bouncing into the safety nets because they couldn't do it.

"Lila, you're nearly there," said Bella, encouragingly. "Just remember the order, fly, fold wings, forward roll, open wings and fly. Try it again."

There was a wonderful moment when Lila did just that, almost by accident.

Practice Makes Perfect

"Did you see?" she cried, but then she couldn't do it again.

"But you will," said Bella. And Bella was right, for after two more sessions Lila could turn somersaults whenever she wanted.

"That's fantastic," said Bella. "Bee Balm and Sea Holly can't somersault like that. And Bee Balm's always puffing and taking rests. Haven't you noticed?"

Lila was thrilled to be able to somersault but her spirits plummeted when she thought that the rest of the class would be flying by themselves long before she was.

In between lessons and flying practice, Lila spent a lot of time perfecting the ventriloquism charm. She still thought it might come in useful and was determined to be as good at it as Bee Balm. She wanted to be able to throw her voice to the top of a tree and, even more difficult, send it behind one. She felt she was succeeding when she hid under her bed and sent her voice into the wardrobe. Meggie and Bella opened the wardrobe door to look for her, believing she was stuck inside. When Lila burst out laughing, they hauled her from under the bed and tickled her in revenge.

But somersaulting and being a good ventriloquist was one thing; try as she might, after six solid days of thinking about it, Lila had no idea how to get Bee Balm and Sea Holly to admit they had tricked her.

The evening before the Flying Test, Lila felt particularly miserable. After all the practice she was certain she could pass her first try. She was even confident about turning somersaults. But by the end of the final practice Meggie still hadn't managed to complete a single one.

Back in their bedroom, Meggie slumped despairingly onto her bed.

"My only comfort is that when you take the

test, Lila, I will be retaking it with you," Meggie said. "I'll never pass the first time; no somersaults, no pass."

"It's tension," said Bella. "You've got to relax into the roll."

"That's what Musk Mallow says," Meggie agreed. "I just don't seem to be able to do it."

"We can't let you fail," said Lila, jumping onto her bed. "Try this!" She balanced herself on the headboard, dived forward onto the mattress in a perfect roll, and landed on her toes before bouncing onto her bottom.

"I can't do that," wailed Meggie. "I'll crush my wings."

"Not if you keep them folded," said Lila.

"Go on, Meggie, give it a try," said Bella. "You can't hurt yourself. The beds are nice and bouncy."

Meggie hesitated.

"After you've done it once you'll wonder why you didn't do it earlier," said Lila. "Bella and I will

Ready to Fly

stand on either side of you to make sure you don't bounce off."

"It's now or never," said Bella. "You've gotten so much better at everything else, you can't fail because of this."

Meggie balanced on the headboard.

"Somersault or bust," she said, between gritted teeth.

"After three," said Lila. "One, two, three – go!"

After the briefest hesitation, Meggie rolled over and landed on her bottom. Lila and Bella cheered. Meggie sat up, surprised. "Did I go over?"

"Did you go over?" said Lila. "Yes, you did. That was your first somersault."

"Do another one," said Bella. "Right away so you remember how it feels."

Meggie did another, this time with more enthusiasm, and landed on her toes before bouncing backward onto her bottom.

Practice Makes Perfect

"And again," smiled Lila.

Five somersaults later and even Meggie was laughing. "I can't believe it's that easy. It feels safe with the bed to bounce on and you two there. I wish you could do the test with me, Lila. Who'll be my partner for the trapeze exchange and the somersaults, if I can't have you?"

"Me," said Bella. "I've already asked Musk Mallow. She was going to put you with Primrose, but I can partner you and Primrose no probs."

"Oh, Bella, thank you," said Meggie. "But I so wish it could have been Lila."

"Me too," said Bella. The mood changed and all three fairies sat glumly on their beds.

Lila held her little unicorn charm between her fingers. It glinted in the light and she was sure she felt it give a teeny little tingle.

"I wish I could make my unicorn come to life," she sighed. "Bella, have you any ideas?"

"If I did, I'd be using them to get my hat charm

onto my head. At least you know you can ride a unicorn. I'll have to wear my charm if I can ever magic it to life."

"My silver scissors charm will be for cutting," said Meggie.

"But for cutting what?" said Bella.

"Paper and fabric," said Meggie, surprised. "Isn't that what scissors usually cut?"

"Maybe," said Bella. "But school first charms do extraordinary things. It won't be any old boring pair of scissors."

"I suppose not," said Meggie. "But tapping them with my wand doesn't magic them, I've tried."

"If only it were that easy," said Bella. "After a whole year I still can't get my hat charm to work. I've almost stopped trying."

"Do you realize," said Lila, making an effort to be cheerful. "We'll have earned fifteen charms by the time we leave school, then, add our own special first day charm, and we'll have sixteen in all. Think of that! Our bracelets will jangle just like Fairy Godmother Whimbrel's."

"And Pipity's," Meggie added.

"Speak for yourselves," said Bella. "I've managed to go a whole year without earning a single one." Then she added. "So far!"

"That's more like it," said Lila.

Bella flew to the windowsill, her favorite seat, where she sat silently musing until something outside caught her eye.

"Hey, you two, guess who I can see? Our royal Princess and her favorite friend are sneaking toward the Wishing Wood. Now why would they be going there this late in the day?"

"For a walk?" suggested Meggie.

"When it's starting to get dark? I don't think so," said Bella. "No, no, no, I think they might be heading for the Flutter Tower for a little last-minute practice. Their somersaults have been useless."

Ready to Fly

"They wouldn't!" said Meggie.

"I'm only guessing," said Bella, opening the window for a better look.

"Let me see. Is Marigold with them?" asked Lila.

"No," said Bella. "They're on their own. If Marigold knew she'd be furious."

"They're looking over their shoulders to see if anyone's following them," said Lila. "Now they're running for cover in the wood." Lila's silver unicorn gave a little jump. This time she knew what he meant – be careful.

"I'm going to find out what they're up to," said Bella. "Anyone coming with me?" Without waiting for a reply, she flew out of the window.

"Butterburs and bodkins!" said Lila. "We can't let her go on her own."

"But what can we do?" asked Meggie. "We're not allowed to fly."

"We've got to go after her," said Lila. "Before something unfortunate happens."

Ready to Fly

"I'm going to find Musk Mallow," said Meggie. "I don't want either of you getting into more trouble."

Both fairies hurried into the common room. There was no sign of Musk Mallow and no one seemed to know where she was. Lila and Meggie hurried out of the Star Clan turret and ran down the great Owl staircase to the Hall of Rainbows. Musk Mallow was nowhere to be seen.

"Meggie, you find her," said Lila. "I'm going after Bella. You know how impulsive she can be. I don't want her to do something she'll regret."

"I'll be as quick as I can," said Meggie.

Lila pulled open the great door that led into the garden and went out into the night. She searched the shadows for signs of life but could see no one. The trees of the Wishing Wood looked dark and scary in the fading light. Nevertheless, Bella was in the wood somewhere, and Lila set off to find her.

Chapter Eight

The Flutter Tower at Night

It was even darker at the edge of the Wishing Wood. Lila glanced back up at the many glowing windows in the castle and noticed, too, the golden light that came from Captain Klop's room at the gatehouse. The path ahead was black and forbidding. An owl hoot made her jump. It seemed to say "Keep out." Lila took a deep breath and, with a wary eye, slipped between the trees.

She listened cautiously and peered through the gloom. There were no voices, only the occasional

Ready to Fly

rustle, perhaps a creature settling down for the night or stirring in its sleep. The owl hooted again, further off this time, as though it had lost interest in her. Her courage grew and she moved faster between the trees, treading lightly, taking care not to snap any twigs.

Ahead she could make out the dark shape of the oak that marked where the path split. She took the right-hand fork, as she had done on so many previous visits to the Flutter Tower, but she'd never felt scared here before.

The owl hooted a third time, almost overhead. In a panic Lila leaped behind a tree and hid. She kept as still as a frightened mouse.

"Found you!" A hand on her shoulder made Lila almost die of fright.

"It's only me!"

"Bella!" Lila said. "What do you think you're doing?"

"Didn't you hear my owl hoots? They were

The Flutter Tower at Night

to encourage you to keep going. Where's Meggie?"

"Gone to find Musk Mallow," said Lila, trying to recover herself. "She's worried we're going to get into trouble."

"Bee Balm and Sea Holly are searching for the Flutter Tower," said Bella, ignoring the idea of trouble as if it was of no importance. "And they're lost in the dark. It's really funny."

"They don't know the woods as well as you do," said Lila.

"They don't know the woods at all. Let's catch up to them." Bella took Lila's hand and pulled her on a winding route through the trees. They moved so fast that Lila quickly lost her bearings.

"Please, slow down. Going this fast is scary. I keep expecting to crash into something."

"Sorry," said Bella. "But we're nearly there now. Listen."

They hid behind a stout tree trunk and

peeked out. Bee Balm's voice was loud enough for them to hear every word.

"For goodness' sake, Sea Holly, you said we were going the right way."

"I thought we were! It's too dark to see anything."

"Can't you do a light charm or something?" snapped Bee Balm. "This is ridiculous."

"You mean the Lord Chamberlain didn't teach you one? He taught you everything else."

"He didn't need to, stupid. It's always light in the Fairy Palace."

"There's no need to get snippy with me!"

Sea Holly had barely finished speaking when the moon slipped out from behind the clouds and the silver wall of the Flutter Tower glinted brightly in front of them.

"Hey, we were here all along," said Bee Balm, her mood quickly changing.

Bella took Lila's hand again and they crept

The Flutter Tower at Night

closer until they could see both fairies looking up at the top of the tower.

"You go first, Sea Holly, and make sure there's no one in there. Then tell me if it's all clear," Bee Balm ordered. Sea Holly hesitated. "Go on."

"Bee Balm is unbelievably bossy," whispered Bella. "I wouldn't go if she told me like that."

"Can't we fly up together?" Sea Holly asked. "I don't want to go in by myself."

"Don't be a baby," said Bee Balm. "Off you go."

"I don't have to take orders from you," huffed Sea Holly.

"If you want to stay my friend, you do."

"Now they're really going to argue," said Bella, relishing the thought.

"No, I don't think so," said Lila. "Sea Holly always does what she's told in the end."

With an enormous sigh, Sea Holly took off, her wings glittering blue in the moonlight.

"I'm going after her," whispered Bella. "I'll

Ready to Fly

pretend to be a ghost. What an opportunity! I'll try out the ventriloquist charm for real."

"Don't go into the Flutter Tower or you'll get into trouble. And don't let Bee Balm see you," whispered Lila, as Bella took off and disappeared into the branches above.

Bee Balm paced up and down, swishing her fairy frock and tossing her long pink hair. Then she stood, hands on her hips, and glared up at the tower, her foot tapping impatiently. She didn't hear the snuffle and rustle of something moving gently toward her. Lila peered into the dark shadows between the trees. Whatever could it be?

A long, rippling shape crawled into a pool of moonlight; a hundred little booted feet working in perfect rhythm. Lila smiled. It was the long-lost wellipede from the game of Bugs and Butterflies. It must have been very shortsighted because it bumped into the Princess. Bee Balm yelped, tripped and dropped her wand in alarm. But it wasn't only the Princess who was frightened – the wellipede was terrified too. It had lost at least ten of its little boots. As it started pulling them on again the Princess fluttered hither and thither searching for her wand.

"You stupid bug!" she shouted, at last. "You're sitting on it!"

This, Lila realized, was her chance. She touched her lips with her wand and flicked her wrist. "Yes, yes," the unicorn on her bracelet seemed to say as it jumped up and down. It knew exactly what she was going to do. She gave a little cough and began.

"Why don't you help me put my boots on, little fairy?" Lila said, listening delightedly. The words were perfectly timed, and it looked exactly as if the wellipede had spoken.

"What...what did you say?" The Princess stared in disbelief and the wellipede looked up at her.

"I've got to put all my boots back on before I can get up."

Ready to Fly

The horrified Princess took two steps backward and fluttered into the nearest tree. She stared down warily from her branch. The bug lifted up sorrowful eyes.

"You know, you're a very clever fairy!" the wellipede continued. "Being able to throw your voice and everything. That Lilac Blossom was completely fooled the other day."

"What? What are you talking about?" Bee Balm asked.

The wellipede rolled its eyes and turned its head this way and that, trying to work out why there was a voice coming from its mouth. But the movements made the wellipede look as though it was about to tell a secret and was checking to make sure that no one else was listening.

"Lilac Blossom totally believed Nutmeg was stuck in the tree. You fooled her good and proper. I saw it all."

Now it was Princess Bee Balm's turn to look

this way and that. "I did fool her, didn't I?" she whispered, with a pleased smile. "But I'd appreciate it if you didn't mention it to anyone else."

Lila nearly gave herself away with a whoop of joy. The Princess had admitted the trick. If only Musk Mallow had been there to hear what Bee Balm had said.

Lila knew she ought to send the wellipede back to the silver sunflower, but she also knew that as long as it was sitting on the Princess's wand, Bee Balm wouldn't dare come down from the tree.

The problem was, the wellipede only had three more boots to put on before it could scuttle off again. She had no idea how to keep it there.

"How did you learn that voice-throwing trick?" the wellipede asked. Lila was getting desperate; two boots to go.

"From my friend the Lord Chamberlain," replied the Princess. "It's a ventriloquism charm.

The Flutter Tower at Night

It's really, really hard to do. I've been practicing it for ages." The bug struggled with the last boot.

"Must have been easy to outwit that stupid Lilac Blossom?"

"Easy as winking," said the Princess. "She has no brains at all."

The boot was on. Lila darted forward and touched the bug's tail with her wand. The wellipede disappeared with a pop and a spray of purple stars, gone to the silver sunflower. Lila picked up Bee Balm's wand.

"Yours, I believe," she said, using her bug voice and making it come from beside Bee Balm on the branch.

"Eeek!" squeaked Bee Balm, almost falling out of the tree with shock. But seeing the wellipede wasn't beside her she looked down. "Oh! Oh, no! Lilac Blossom, it's you," she cried out in alarm. "H-h-have you just gotten here, by any chance?"

Ready to Fly

Lila's reply was interrupted by a fearful yell that came from the top of the Flutter Tower. Bee Balm sat bolt upright. "What…what was that?" asked the Princess, before fluttering a little higher up the tree. Lila spun around, a wand in each hand, wondering the same thing. It was at that moment that Captain Klop limped out from between the trees. Lila had never been so pleased to see anyone in her life.

"Captain Klop, did you hear that cry?" she asked.

"I think the whole school did," replied the old dragon.

The words were barely out of his mouth when Sea Holly dived to the ground and landed in a trembling heap.

"There's a ghost! There's a ghost! It's chasing me!"

"No, there isn't," said Bella, dropping down beside her. "It was me, just little me, pretending to be a ghost. Woooo wooo, wooo!"

The Flutter Tower at Night

"Ghosts! I shouldn't be finding fairies playing silly games at this time of night," said Captain Klop, frowning. "But I'd be interested to know why you're all out here when you should be safely tucked up in bed." But before he could question them further whirring wings distracted him. "And now who's coming?"

It was Musk Mallow, dashing between the trees, followed by a galaxy of spinning orange suns: she had brought Mistress Pipit with her.

"Whatever's going on here?" Mistress Pipit demanded. "And whose pink wand is that, Lilac Blossom?"

"Bee Balm's, Mistress Pipit," said Lila, bobbing a curtsy.

"And where is the Princess may I ask?" Mistress Pipit's tones were icy.

Lila glanced up but Bee Balm stayed hidden in the tree. "Very well," said Mistress Pipit, tapping the pink wand with her own. It flew from Lila's grasp and shot into the air, leaving a trail of orange suns. "It's no use hiding, Bee Balm, I know where you are. Fairies who are foolish enough to lose their wands can always be found. Come down at once."

There was a moment's silence and then Bee Balm fluttered from the tree and stood defiantly in front of her teacher. "And what were you doing up there?" The Princess fiddled with her bracelet but said nothing.

Mistress Pipit turned to Sea Holly with an angry swirl. "Explain what's going on, at once, Sea Holly."

Sea Holly was too terrified to think of a lie. "I was seeing if it was all clear for Bee Balm and me to practice in the Flutter Tower." Bee Balm glared at her.

"Were you now?" said Mistress Pipit. "And Lilac Blossom, how do you and Harebell fit into all this?"

The Flutter Tower at Night

"We saw Bee Balm and Sea Holly sneaking toward the Wishing Wood and, well, we followed them," said Lila.

"I suspected they were going to practice in the Flutter Tower," said Bella. "And I was right."

"And Nutmeg told me what was happening," added Musk Mallow. "She didn't want Lilac Blossom to get into any more trouble."

"Very sensible," said Mistress Pipit. "But you are *all* in trouble. No First Year fairy should be in the Wishing Wood at this time of night."

Lila took a deep breath and said quickly, "Bella and I wanted to prove that Bee Balm and Sea Holly tricked me into flying up into the tree. It's been practically the only thing I've thought about since it happened. And I'm glad I followed them. Bee Balm admitted everything to the wellipede."

"I didn't," said Bee Balm. "I told the beastly bug I didn't know what it was talking about."

An interesting silence followed. Bee Balm

looked from one fairy to another wondering what she had said wrong.

"Bee Balm," said Mistress Pipit, "wellipedes can't talk!"

"What do you mean they can't..." The Princess bit her lip and clenched her fists.

"I gave the wellipede a voice," said Lila. "And you told it the truth."

"I did not!" yelled the furious Princess.

"Well, from where I was standing, you did," interjected Captain Klop, stroking his chin with a claw. "You see, Bee Balm, I heard voices and came to find out what was going on. You had an interesting conversation with that bug before Lilac Blossom tapped its tail. You sounded more than pleased to have tricked her into flying into the tree to rescue Nutmeg, with a naughty voice-throwing trick."

"It was nothing to do with me," said Sea Holly, in a panic. "I can't do the ventriloquism charm."

The Flutter Tower at Night

"Now I remember you," said Captain Klop. "You were the blue fairy who sent Lilac Blossom into the Wishing Wood. I watched you from the gatehouse. Lilac Blossom was going in to lunch but you said something that sent her running in a different direction."

"Oh dear," said Mistress Pipit. "It looks as though I've made a terrible mistake. Thank you for the explanation, Captain Klop, and you too, Lilac Blossom. Have you any more denials to make, Bee Balm?" Bee Balm shook her head. "No, I should think not." Mistress Pipit stood thoughtfully for a moment. "Lilac Blossom, I see now that you were tricked into flying up into the tree, and, in turn, I was tricked into punishing you. I said at the time if it had been a genuine rescue I would have been lenient. And I will be now. You will take the Flying Proficiency Test with the rest of the class tomorrow and I will return your six clan points. Also, I'll give you an extra six to make up for the miserable time you must have had over the last few days."

Lila, overwhelmed with relief, curtsied deeply. Mistress Pipit smiled kindly at her, but the smile quickly faded as she turned her attention to Bee Balm and Sea Holly. "As for you two," she said, "I will not have such mean-spirited and outrageous rule-breaking in my class. Your wands, please."

Aghast, Bee Balm and Sea Holly put their wands into Mistress Pipit's outstretched hand. "These are confiscated until further notice and neither of you will take the Flying Test tomorrow. You will return to the Sun Clan with me right now."

Mistress Pipit touched each fairy's shoulder and the three of them disappeared in a shower of golden suns.

Musk Mallow turned to Lila and Bella. "Now then, you two," she said. "Time for bed."

"Thank you, Captain Klop," whispered Lila, as they turned to leave. The great dragon nodded down at her and gave her purple hair a gentle pat, before continuing his patrol through the wood. Bella took Lila's hand and Musk Mallow gave her a grin before leading the way back to school.

"Well done, Lilac Blossom," smiled Musk Mallow. "Pass the Flying Test tomorrow and you might make the Bugs and Butterflies practice after all."

Lila couldn't quite believe what had happened. She had actually made Bee Balm tell the truth. It had been worth all the time it had taken to perfect the ventriloquism charm. She felt free and happy for the first time in days and comforted to know she had a friend in Captain Klop. But the most wonderful thing of all was that she and Meggie could take the Flying Test together. Lila couldn't wait to tell her friend. All they had to do now was pass it.

Chapter Nine

The Test

The following day was one of great excitement. By the time the Charm One fairies arrived for their first lesson, they were buzzing with tales of what had happened in the Wishing Wood the previous night. The fairies were also nervous about taking the Flying Proficiency Test later that morning. Even Bella was tense and she was only helping out.

As the pupils filed into class Princess Bee Balm arrived with her face set, pretending that nothing

The Test

was wrong, but Sea Holly was miserable and she couldn't hide it from anyone. Mistress Pipit made both fairies come out and face the class and then she asked Lila to remain standing by her mushroom desk at the back.

On Mistress Pipit's command Bee Balm looked Lila straight in the eye and said, "I apologize for tricking you into flying, Lilac Blossom." Lila dropped a half curtsy in response. She couldn't tell whether it was a genuine apology or not.

"And I'm sorry I told you Meggie was stuck in the tree when she wasn't," added Sea Holly, blushing to the roots of her blue hair.

"Thank you, Bee Balm and thank you, Sea Holly," said Mistress Pipit. "Let that be the end of such nasty tricks. Back to your places, please."

The class quickly learned that Bee Balm and Sea Holly's punishment was severe. They were to spend hours in detention and weren't allowed to take the Flying Proficiency Test until retake day in two weeks' time. They were banned from any practice classes in the Flutter Tower for a week and their wands had been confiscated until further notice.

"We've got to pass today," said Lila, upon hearing this. "It would be terrible to have to take the test again with those two."

"I agree," said Meggie. "We will do our very best." Lila gave her friend a beaming smile.

A little while later the class had assembled in their clan groups inside the Flutter Tower and were ready to begin. Lila and Meggie were both nervous. The test was going to take all of their concentration. Mistress Pipit waved her wand and, in a flurry of orange stars, an elegant but comfy chair appeared. Everyone knew it was for Fairy Godmother Whimbrel and, when she glided in through the open door, escorted by Day Lily and the four Head of Clan fairies, the tension mounted. The Headteacher settled down to watch with Day Lily at her side.

The Test

"The clans will go in the following order," announced Mistress Pipit. "Clouds, Moons, Suns and Stars."

The Stars groaned at having to go last but Bella said, "That's good. You've got lots of opportunity to learn from the other fairies' mistakes."

"And to get even more nervous," said Lila. "I'd rather get it over and done with."

"Don't be silly," whispered Bella. "It couldn't be better."

"The clan leaders will decide who'll go first in each of their groups," Mistress Pipit continued. "Your points will be recorded on this parchment by me and Fairy Godmother Whimbrel." A scroll appeared in a cascade of brilliant suns and she held it up for all to see. "Each score is out of a hundred. You need sixty points to pass. Those with eighty points and above will gain a distinction."

"Bella," whispered Lila, an interesting thought

Ready to Fly

popping into her head. "Did you get a distinction in your Flying Test by any chance?"

Bella beamed. "I did, as it happens."

"Why didn't you tell us?" said Meggie.

Bella shrugged, modestly. "I didn't want to boast."

Lila and Meggie looked at one another astonished. "Actually," Bella went on. "I did really but Musk Mallow said I should hush up about it. She thought it might worry you. Are you worried?"

"Impressed, more like," said Lila.

"Shush, you three," said Musk Mallow. "Now pay attention everyone, this is the order in which the Star fairies will take the test. First, Cowslip followed by Periwinkle. You'll each do the first five parts of the test. Then straight after Periwinkle finishes, you'll do the pairs maneuvers together. Next, Primrose. Harebell will do the pairs maneuvers with you, Primrose. After that, Nutmeg followed by Lilac Blossom. You two will be the last

The Test

pair of all. Take it slowly and steadily and don't panic. Good luck, everyone."

The Stars settled down to watch the other clans. They had plenty of time to wait. *Look and learn*, Lila told herself. The first fairy to go was Candytuft. She stood with anxious eyes waiting for the signal to start. Mistress Pipit nodded to Angelica, head of the Cloud Clan.

"Ready, Candytuft?" asked Angelica. The fairy nodded. "Make sure you listen out for my counting. Ready, set, go!"

Candytuft flew into the air and spiraled up through the Flutter Tower toward the silver branches at the top, where she perched and waited for the signal to come down. *I'm going to try really hard to go up straight*, thought Lila. *Candytuft is good but I want to go up without the slightest spiral*. At the signal, Candytuft fluttered back to the ground. Then off she went again, this time to the handholds on the wall where she froze so that not a wing tip moved. At Angelica's signal Candytuft dived: one, two, three seconds later, she opened her wings and landed on the floor. Next she flew back to the trapeze where she swung high, jumped free and hovered for a count of five, before folding her wings and dropping down to the ladder. Here she slipped and had to use her hands to steady herself. There was a groan from the Cloud Clan members.

"She didn't position herself directly above the ladder," Lila whispered. "We must remember to get in the right position when we do that." Meggie nodded, keeping her eyes on Candytuft.

A ball dropped from the hole in the ceiling and Candytuft caught it – just. She managed to hang on and send it back into the air. Then she flew to the end of the rope and knotted it to the ladder. She had to hold on to the ladder twice to keep her balance while she hovered, but she managed the knot.

The Test

"She's rushing," whispered Meggie. Lila agreed. "We must remember there's no time limit. Slow but sure."

Candytuft's relief was obvious once that part of the test was over, and her partner, Coral Flower, began. Coral Flower was slightly less nervous than Candytuft, although she did slip off the wall and failed to catch the ball first time. Then the two fairies flew up for the difficult part, the swing on the trapeze with the twist-leap to change places, followed by the midair meeting and the two somersaults to earth, holding hands. They managed the twist-leap and one somersault before their hands came apart. But they had done well and landed to a round of applause.

Lila and Meggie concentrated hard as the rest of the class followed one after another. At last, after a long wait, it was the Stars' turn to go. Lila became really anxious watching Cowslip, then Periwinkle work their way through the test. She squeezed

Ready to Fly

Meggie's hand and Meggie's return squeeze steadied her nerves. Cowslip and Periwinkle did well although they didn't quite manage to complete the two somersaults. Primrose did a good test too until the somersaults, when, even with Bella's help, she could only manage one, before pulling her hand away to land. Then it was Meggie's turn.

"Good luck," whispered Lila, thinking how difficult those two somersaults were.

Meggie took off. She spiraled a little as she flew up, but not too badly, and she didn't get frightened even when she looked down. Lila breathed a sigh of relief. After her extra practice with Musk Mallow, Meggie seemed to be coping with her fear of heights. She completed all the maneuvers well, until the hover, when she had to grab the ladder to balance in order to knot the rope. Back on the ground she looked mightily relieved.

"Good luck," she whispered to Lila.

"Go for it," said Bella. Lila focused herself.

The Test

Passing the test had become more important than she could ever have imagined. She stood on tiptoes and raised her wings in readiness.

"One, two, three, go!" said Musk Mallow.

Lila took off. It was the best vertical flight she had ever managed and she landed comfortably on the nearest silver branch, pleased to have made a good beginning. She waited for the signal and flew down again. *Not too bad so far*, she thought.

Flying back to the wall, she clasped the handholds and froze, hardly daring to blink, waiting for Musk Mallow's signal. When it came she pitched herself forward into a dive, one, two, three, the floor was coming up fast. At the last minute, she opened her wings, straightened up and landed with a gentle bounce. Then straight back up to the trapeze, swing, swing, swing and let go. She steadied herself and hovered to a count of five, exactly above the ladder. Folding her wings, she dropped down, landing with hardly a wobble. Now her eyes were on the silver tree above her. Down came the ball. She caught it and, with the same flowing movement, tossed it back into the air. Next she flew to the rope and carried the end across to the ladder. Keeping her balance in a steady hover, she knotted it carefully. That done she fluttered back to the ground where Meggie was waiting. Together they flew to the trapeze bars.

"Take it steady," said Lila. "No rushing. We must be perfectly balanced before we jump."

They settled themselves on the bars and swung backward and forward, making a bigger arc with each swing, until their toes were almost touching. On the next swing, they looked each other in the eye, Lila nodded, and they jumped, twisted and landed on the opposite bar. It was a perfect exchange. *Now for the real challenge*, thought Lila. They swung toward each other, and slipping from the trapeze bars they clasped hands. They hovered to get their balance.

Ready to Fly

"We can do this, Meggie," said Lila. "It'll be just like somersaulting on the bed. Ready?"

"Yes!"

They rolled forward and turned their first somersault. Over they went again and completed the second somersault. Then, straightening up, they landed side by side, still holding hands. A terrific round of applause greeted them.

"We did it," said Lila, wrapping her arms around Meggie in the biggest hug. Bella couldn't stop jumping up and down, she was so pleased. It took a few minutes for everyone to calm down.

Now the class had to wait patiently, while Mistress Pipit and Fairy Godmother Whimbrel conferred, with the help of Day Lily. It seemed like an age before the results were read out. It was so exciting; fairy after fairy had passed. It took ages to get to the Stars but, at last, it was their turn.

"Cowslip, pass," read out Mistress Pipit.

The Test

"Periwinkle, pass, Primrose, pass, Nutmeg, pass."
Lila bit her lip. She could hardly breathe. "And
last but not least, Lilac Blossom." There was a
pause. "Pass with distinction." Lila gasped. Bella
gave her a hug, Meggie kissed her cheek and there
was a huge cheer. Lila could hardly believe it. Pass
with distinction! It was beyond her imaginings.

"Well done all of you," Mistress Pipit said, with
a pleased smile. "I'm extremely proud of you.
Now off you go. Have a good fly around the
Wishing Wood with your friends. Head of Clan
fairies accompany them, please. Enjoy yourselves."

"Bee Balm's going to turn from pink to green
when she finds out you've got a distinction," said
Bella. "Especially after all the detentions she's got
to do."

"Don't let's think about that just now,"
said Lila.

Meggie agreed. "No more fear of heights for
me, I hope. Let's fly!"

Ready to Fly

The door to the Flutter Tower opened but Bella was already leading the way upward toward the silver branches and the opening beyond. Lila and Meggie hurried to catch up. What more could they want than to fly out into the Wishing Wood and play among the trees? Fairy after fairy followed them up, a glittering array of fluttering wings in the sunlight.

"Come on," called Bella to her two friends, as they burst out from the Flutter Tower. "Let's fly. Whoopee!"

"Well done, Stars, and very well done, Lilac Blossom," called Musk Mallow, as they flew off. "See you all at the Bugs and Butterflies practice. Don't be late!"

As if we would be, thought Lila. She could hardly believe she had passed the Flying Proficiency Test with distinction. *I'll have to write another letter home*, she thought. *Cook will be so proud.*

"I've passed," Lila told the little silver unicorn

The Test

on her bracelet. "And one day we'll fly together even higher and faster than I can fly now."

Lila was overjoyed to be flying free above the Wishing Wood with her two best friends. And tomorrow they would practice Bugs and Butterflies for the first time. Lila was looking forward to it so much she could hardly wait. Silverlake Fairy School was the best place to be. Without a doubt, she was the happiest fairy in the whole world.

Join Lila and her friends
for more magical adventures at

Silverlake
Fairy School

Unicorn Dreams

Lila longs to go to Silverlake Fairy School to learn about wands, charms and fairy magic – but spoiled Princess Bee Balm is set on ruining Lila's chances! Luckily nothing can stop Lila from following her dreams...

Wands and Charms

It's Lila's first day at Silverlake Fairy School, and she's delighted to receive her first fairy charm and her own wand. But Lila quickly ends up breaking the school rules when bossy Princess Bee Balm gets her into trouble. Could Lila's school days be numbered...?

 # Stardust Surprise

Stardust is the most magical element in the fairy world. Although the fairies are allowed to experiment with it in lessons, stardust is so powerful that they are forbidden to use it by themselves. But Princess Bee Balm will stop at nothing to boost her magic...

Bugs and Butterflies

Bugs and Butterflies is the magical game played at Silverlake Fairy School. Lila dreams of being picked to play for her clan's team, and she has a good chance too, until someone starts cheating. Princess Bee Balm is also being unusually friendly to Lila...so what's going on?

Dancing Magic

It's the end of term at Silverlake Fairy School, and Lila and her friends are practicing to put on a spectacular show. There's a wonderful surprise in store for Lila too – one she didn't dare dream was possible!

For more fairy fun, fly to

www.silverlakefairyschool.com

About the Author

Elizabeth Lindsay trained as a drama teacher before becoming a puppeteer on children's television. Elizabeth has published over thirty books, as well as writing numerous radio and television scripts including episodes of *The Hoobs*. Elizabeth dreams up adventures for Lilac Blossom from her attic in Gloucestershire, where she enjoys fairytale views down to the River Severn valley. If Elizabeth could go to Silverlake Fairy School, she would like a silver wand with a star at its tip, as she'd hope to be with Lila in the Star Clan. Like Lila, Elizabeth's favorite color is purple.